AGNES MOOR'S WILD KNIGHT

Alyssa Cole

AGNES MOOR'S WILD KNIGHT

BOOKS BY ALYSSA COLE

Historicals:
Agnes Moor's Wild Knight
Be Not Afraid
The Brightest Day (anthology)

Off the Grid series:
Radio Silence
Signal Boost
Mixed Signals

Standalones:
Eagle's Heart
Sweet to the Taste

ACKNOWLEDGMENTS

I'd like to thank Julia Kelly and Lena Hart for being spectacular friends and sounding boards. You're both wonderful.

I'd also like to thank my main writing crew: Katana Collins, Derek Bishop, and Krista Amigone. Your support and feedback is invaluable, even when video chat programs try to keep us apart.

For my mother, Earline, who passed on her love of romance in general and Highlanders in particular to me.

"There she is!" an excited voice called out across the crowded tourney grounds. "Agnes Moor!"

Ah, so it's Moor today, Agnes thought with a twinge of resentment. That was what they called her when they were feeling good-natured. It was Agnes Black when they wanted to stress that she wasn't one of them, as if her umber skin and cap of short, tight curls weren't reminder enough. But today was the final day of the tourney, a time for gaiety and celebration, so Moor it was.

Agnes swallowed the nervous sickness, or perhaps motion sickness, rising in her throat and gripped the arms of the chaise triumphal as it rocked to and fro. Each step the two brawny squires hefting her gilded seat took across the tournament grounds brought her closer to being tipped right out of the chair. She was lithe despite her height, so she wasn't very heavy, but the chair was; the last thing she needed was to be pitched into one of the mounds of horse muck scattered across the packed dirt. She felt foolish enough as it was, being paraded around like no more than a box of crowns to be handed out to the victor.

Beneath her dangling slippers, people of every strata surged around the food and trinket stalls, haggling over imported fruit and fabrics. Conjurers, James's latest obsession, displayed their dark magicks in bursts of flame and elaborate sleights of hand. Agnes knew it was all deception, but the wild-haired men with black robes and ink etched into their pale skin frightened her, just a bit. All around her, the wonders of James IV's world-renowned court were writ large; the elaborate displays reflected those things that intrigued the king at the moment. His interests were many and varied, and thank God for that or Agnes would never have set foot in his court, let alone become a part of it.

She heard the innuendo-loaded whispers from the crowd in her wake: those were a constant part of her life in Scotland. Some said she had been rescued from a Portuguese slave ship that foundered on Scotland's shores. Others thought she was a changeling child, left by the dark Sidhe. The king preferred the story that Agnes was an African princess who had joined the other "exotics" in his court—the Italian alchemists, the Moorish dancers, the Spanish mathematicians—of her own accord. Her father, now just a faded memory, had called her his little queen, and that was the very closest she came to nobility, but Agnes much preferred James's narrative to her true past. And after three days of being carried around the court, she was starting to feel a bit royal. Luckily for her, the charade was almost over.

"Oh, do take care!" she cried out as her porters stumbled and nearly dropped her into a troop of thespians. The actors were reenacting the previous day's glorious display by the Wild Knight. The jouster had gained the appellation because he won every match through a combination of brute strength and intelligent maneuvering, paired with the intensity of a berserker. The fact that he refused to reveal his identity made him even more appealing to the crowds. Just thinking of the mysterious rider who thrashed even the most accomplished jousters, of what his feats represented, sent a thrill of heat through her.

He is coming for you. The feverish thought had been seared into Agnes's brain since she'd seen him rout his first opponent. It disturbed her, this discordant emotion. She'd felt such a draw only once before, and having finally rid herself of the foolish fantasies that meeting produced, she wasn't eager to relive the experience. Desiring a man you shouldn't was one thing; desiring one whom you hadn't even seen was quite another.

As the squires carried Agnes through the crowd, the mass of people parted like the sea, allowing her passage but then closing in on all sides, engulfing the space around her feet as they shouted their encouragement. Some tried to touch her skin to see if it somehow felt different from their own. Agnes wondered if they expected scales; she tucked her feet up under the chaise. Other people fingered the elaborate golden cloak that she wore draped over her gem-green gown, both of which had been bestowed upon her by the king himself. She thought of the cloak as her own suit of armor against this grabbing, staring crowd, which was a bit paradoxical as this tourney was being held in her honor. At least, she was told it was an honor.

The knight who won the Tournament of the Black Lady would be rewarded with a kiss from the titular woman herself. Agnes, a favorite of the king and queen both, had been chosen for the role. The first such tourney had occurred the year prior, but the Moorish woman who had been championed then was now married and great with child, something Agnes tried not to envy.

It stung a bit to be proffered as a prize, but she knew that James had good intentions. If she could help him smooth relations with the Highland clans by playing this role, she would. He'd saved her life, and more than that, he treated her as an equal—as equal as any king could treat a commoner, of course. For that, Agnes would help him, and her adopted country, however she could.

As the squires carried her toward the dais where Queen Margaret sat with her coterie of handmaidens, Agnes felt a sense of awareness surge through her. She knew before she turned, could feel it in her skin and sinew and someplace much more base, that the gaze of the Wild Knight was upon her. For the past three days, the mysterious man had plowed through the competition, championing Agnes as if the prize were gold or land instead of a simple meeting of lips. Agnes told herself the Wild Knight simply sought acclaim, but after every victory, the dark headpiece of his armor would turn her way, and the same heady sensation of being watched by hungry eyes would streak through her.

He rode a destrier of darkest black that matched the matte metal of his armor. Agnes couldn't help but notice how large and broad the sculpted metal was. If it had been tailored to the man inside, he was exceptionally built indeed.

You've only met one man that large in all your travels. The thought threatened her with a spark of hope that simply couldn't be. Only noblemen were allowed to joust in these tourneys, not Highland clansmen, so she would likely be stuck kissing some toady baron or earl.

When her chair was settled onto the ground, finally, she only had a moment to get her bearing before the whinny of a horse and the raising of the hairs on her neck alerted her to his presence behind her. When she turned, the destrier was trotting up to the dais. A youth with a shock of red hair sporting a green and yellow plaid walked alongside the great beast, looking as if he had been given an assignment of great import. Agnes focused on him instead of the armored hulk atop the horse.

He bowed gracefully for such a gangly youth, and then spoke in English. "My lord requests a favor of the maiden Agnes before he enters this final match, against a noble adversary. A strip of fabric to fly from his lance."

Agnes raised a brow at the boy and the sharp blade he held in his hand, and then turned her gaze to the Wild Knight, who loomed over her from atop his steed. What man hid beneath that well-worn metal suit?

"I rather like this dress," she replied in Gaelic. "And I rather dislike mending, so I must decline his favor."

The man seemed immobile, but the horse shifted, as if responding to some change disguised by the great suit of armor. Agnes felt a spark of anger within her. Perhaps he thought his attentions flattering, but they simply made her the object of even more speculation. She'd heard one of the visiting knights, an English oaf who had been unseated in a trice, speculate as she passed him the day before. *Does the Moorish maid wield some particular talent with her mouth that the Wild Knight fights so fervently for her kiss?*

Agnes flushed with anger at the memory, but pushed the thought from her mind. The Wild Knight had spent the past three days disconcerting her. Was it not fair that she should do the same when given the opportunity?

"I should take offense, Sir Knight. Have you no other source of motivation to win beyond a strip of fabric?" she asked, eyebrows raised. "Is not the favor of my kiss enough for you?"

The youth looked at her with bug eyes and then risked a glance up at his master as if he feared for her life.

"Not nearly enough, sweet Agnes," a deep, rich voice echoed through the vent of the mask. The languid burr exuded power and strength, and Agnes's body reacted instinctively, the tips of her breasts pulling up into tight buds and her sex clenching with awareness. "You shall learn that quite well when I claim my prize."

With that, he wheeled his horse and rode away, his squire scrambling behind him.

When I claim my prize. There was no equivocation there: he meant to win. The sensual promise of his words set off a strange ache low in her belly. Agnes had taken lovers during her time in James's court; she enjoyed the indulgences of the flesh as much as anyone. But those men hadn't made her feel like molten iron on the smithy's anvil with just a few words. Agnes suppressed a shudder at thoughts of what the Wild

Knight could do to her, how his broad, muscled chest would feel pressed against her own...

She shook the thoughts from her head. The man her imagination conjured was not beneath that armor. He was nothing but a fantasy now, a regret, and one that shouldn't be indulged lest she sink even further into the abysmal loneliness that had haunted her since their meeting.

"Do you know the last time I saw a man fight so fiercely for a woman's attentions?" Queen Margaret asked with a knowing smile as she gestured Agnes toward the seat beside her, pulling her from her reverie.

"I think you misunderstand, Your Majesty," Agnes said, feeling exposed as the queen and her maids eyed her curiously. "He fights for prestige at best, or, at worst, to experience a novelty."

Agnes's words rang false, although they echoed the fears that had surfaced as she watched the Wild Knight plow through the competition with single-minded determination. She had always been seen as something of an object instead a person: why would he see her any differently?

"If he sought an exotic kiss, he could ask you directly, or Helena or Mary," Margaret said, mentioning her Moorish maids. "If he sought only prestige, there would not be such power in his blows, as if every contender stood between him and what's rightfully his. No, the last time I saw such intensity in a man was when James courted me, following me to and fro, composing love songs on his lute, taking me out on hunts, and making love to me every second we were alone."

The queen stared into the distance as if recalling a fond memory.

"Your Majesty!" Agnes chided with a scandalized laugh. She knew the king and queen were truly in love, and often wished she could find the same for herself. But such things were not meant for people like her, were they? Hadn't she already diminished her store of luck when she had been welcomed into this court and treated with respect? To expect more from this life would be greed, pure and simple. If she had to forever ignore the yawning gulf of loneliness at the very pit of her, she wouldn't be the first woman to do so.

"This man does not champion that which he could receive for two coins, Agnes. That is plain for anyone to see, especially someone as sharp as you," Margaret said. "I must say, if this is the level of acuity you bring to your dealings with the ambassadors, perhaps James and I were mistaken about you."

The words were said jokingly, but for all that they still stung. Agnes said nothing, though. She decided it was better to play the fool than to acknowledge the Wild Knight's effect on her and prove herself to be one.

The marischal, a peculiar, unkempt man who looked frightening but was always kind to Agnes, stepped before the crowd and read the lists. He spoke for only a few moments but it seemed to drag on forever, as if time had taken on a new dimension preceding this final match. The herald arrived eventually, blowing trills of fanfare from his horn to shoo the marischal away before making the final proclamations and introducing the combatants.

The two contenders took their positions on either side of the field of honor. The other knight, a Frenchman in a sleek suit of armor decorated in a painted floral pattern, had a style that was more theatrical in contrast to the Wild Knight's brute strength, but he was every bit as skilled, and was considered a formidable opponent. He trotted his horse in circles and reveled in the attentions of the crowd. The Wild Knight sat unmoving when his name was called, even though the hum of the people packing the stands rose to a roar. He didn't acknowledge them, simply hefted the weight of his lance in his large hand as if impatient for the match to begin. His vented mask turned in Agnes's direction for a long moment, and the thrill of his gaze passed over her again, raising the hairs on her neck.

The queen leaned toward Agnes so her words would be heard over the earsplitting noise of the crowd. "You may feign ignorance if you wish, but if you do not desire to give this warrior your heart, you had best prepare yourself for battle."

Agnes felt something coil tightly in her chest at Margaret's words, like a trap set for any man who might dally with her emotions. But perhaps the springs on the trap were rusting, because for a moment she allowed herself to wonder if the queen was right. That the man beneath the armor might actually seek more than the prize of a kiss from her. The thought was too frightening to be allowed, and she pushed it away as she did all such impracticalities.

It was time now. The marischal made his signal and the joust began. Agnes heard the deep cry of her champion as the black destrier surged toward his opponent, and was altogether shaken. She wasn't sure she *could* win a battle against him, if it came down to it, or if she even wanted to.

The cries of the crowd gave way to an awed silence broken only by the clatter of hooves on dirt and armor against leather saddle. All eyes were riveted on the men as they stormed toward one another, their skill apparent in the tilt of their lances and the way they seated their horses. Agnes's heart was in her throat as she watched the Wild Knight spur his mount forward. He crouched in the saddle as if he were ready to spring forward and unseat the chevalier using his own body. Instead, at the last moment he swung his heavy lance toward the knight, who tried to parry the blow. For a moment, the two lances locked against each other, brute force matching brute force, but then the Frenchman's lance broke in two and he was dealt a blow straight to his chest.

He was unseated.

The chevalier flew through the air but managed to land in a sprawl that was only slightly ungainly. His squires swarmed him, quickly helping him to his feet. Agnes was surprised he could stand after that terrible hit, but he removed his helmet and gave an ostentatious bow in her direction. She nodded her approval at him—the handsome man had fought valiantly—but her gaze immediately returned to the Wild Knight.

Her heart pounded, galloping as fast as any destrier in the tourney, and she felt as if she would faint from anticipation if he didn't reveal his identity at once. As if he knew how anxious she was, the Wild Knight took his time dismounting. He chatted with his flame-haired squire as the cries of the crowd grew louder and louder, mirroring her own desire to know who he was and what he was about. The tourney was a game, a façade for the real battles, the political ones that were being carried out by dignitaries and statesmen, but something about this moment was all too real. Agnes felt as if her entire life could hinge on the simple lifting of a visor.

Finally, the Wild Knight began to walk toward her with an insouciant swagger that left no doubt that the mystery man grinned beneath his mask. He came to a stop a few feet before the dais and pulled off his helmet. Long obsidian hair unfurled behind him like a banner, and his moss-green gaze locked on to hers, sharp enough to cut to her very soul.

The queen gasped, the handmaidens sighed, and the crowd went wild. Agnes, for her part, was so violently shocked that she leapt to her feet. She barely heard the herald announcing him by his true name, and by the newly added appellation that astonished her even more.

"The winner is Gareth, Clan MacAllister, recently dubbed His Lordship, the Earl of Arran!"

Margaret tugged Agnes back into her seat, presumably so she could gawk in a more dignified manner.

"MacAllister is one of the Highland lairds James parlayed with." The queen couldn't keep the curiosity out of her voice as she continued. "You conversed with him during the visit to seek accord with the clans all those months ago, did you not?"

"Just the once," Agnes managed. Just once, but it had left an indelible mark on her. She'd thought herself foolish—months of pining away for some Highland chief determined to thwart James's plans for unification—but as MacAllister bowed deeply and strode off of the field, she understood that her instinct had been correct: the Wild Knight had come for her.

Maybe once had been enough.

Agnes hadn't wanted to go to the meeting of the Highland chieftains six months before.

She'd known why the king wanted her to accompany him: she was a favorite of the royal couple for a reason, able to discuss both politics and pleasurable pursuits with ease, to soothe ruffled feathers and make sure that the right people spoke to each other in order to further James's goals for Scotland. There was also an unacknowledged, more rankling, reason for her presence: she was an eccentricity that drew people's interest and helped break the ice, like a pet tiger or a dancing bear. In spite of that, Agnes wanted nothing more than to be of use to her adopted country; however, she had been frightened of the arduous journey to MacAllister's keep.

She didn't scare easily, but the rules were different in the far-flung Highlands, mostly in that there weren't any. She was curiosity enough in Edinburgh—in the untamed reaches of Scotland she would be a spectacle, the object of constant attention, and not all of it simple wonder. As the king's entourage had ridden through the encampment that surrounded MacAllister's keep, the crowds comprised of the several clans that had come to hear what the king was about, Agnes had felt the malice rolling off the people. Their defiance, their resistance to Edinburgh rule, was not something that could be changed with a smile and the carefully worded parries she used at court, but she had been determined to try.

The trip had been a failure, to put it kindly. James had spoken with various chieftains, and several of them seemed to tolerate him well enough, but the people of the Highlands didn't wish to find themselves under a king's thumb again. Agnes had done her job, trying to make headway with those chieftains who deigned to acknowledge her, but she had been acutely aware of one man the entire night. The MacAllister.

He was impossible not to notice. He was larger than most of his cohort, but not lumbering or unrefined. There was an exquisite caste to his body that reminded her of the statues chiseled by the Italian artists James had invited to Edinburgh. His impressive musculature couldn't be hidden beneath the tartan he wore, a plaid of green and yellow. Dark hair hung down his back, a few braids along the sides keeping the thick mass from falling into his eyes, which were an impossible shade of green that gave her a flash of the verdant climes of her youth. Agnes knew that of all the men in attendance, he was the one she should be trying to sway—he had the ear of several feuding chieftains who wouldn't deal with each other or with the king—but a different kind of fear had seized her from the moment she'd been introduced to him.

His gaze had followed her intently after their brief encounter, burning into her even as he carried on lively conversations with his political allies. She was accustomed to being stared at, but not in such a way, and certainly not to the reaction MacAllister elicited in her. She'd spent half the night tight with need and hoping for just one dance with him, just one touch of his large hand to the small of her back as they moved synchronously. At the same time, some dueling inner force had screamed that this man was dangerous, that she must avoid him, duty to her king be damned.

She hadn't exchanged more than a greeting with the man, but Agnes hadn't spoken any native tongue when she arrived on Scotland's shores, and she knew what it was to communicate without words. The MacAllister's gaze spoke of possession, of desire. He wanted her, but what frightened her more was the fact that she couldn't be sure her gaze wasn't a mirror of his own. So she had run.

She'd felt like a fool strategically evading him, keeping hulking Highlanders and groups of minstrels and their instruments between them. When the night was drawing to a close and she had successfully kept him at bay, she'd felt a strange mixture of pride and regret. She was sagged against a stone wall in the corner of the great hall, exhausted, when she felt his presence next to her. He leaned against the wall, effectively blocking out the rest of the attendees with the breadth of his back.

"I hope you found everything to your liking, Lady Agnes," he said in a voice that had not lost its thick burr but showed signs of English education. The torchlight danced in his eyes, making him look very much like one of the scullery cats when they cornered their prey. "We're not used to accommodating the likes of the king and his court at my humble keep."

"I've found both the banquet and the accommodations most excellent, Laird MacAllister," she said. She felt completely cowed by his presence, and she hoped it didn't show. "However, I must correct you. I am not a lady, merely a humble emissary of King James's court."

He raised his brows at her words, and then his warm gaze raked over her from head to toe. He may as well have physically run his hands over her for the way Agnes's body reacted. Her blood pulsed and images of the most delicious and inappropriate kind flashed in her mind: MacAllister's mouth on hers, his hands on her breasts, his muscular arms wrapped around her—it was unseemly, her reaction, but she could no more control it than a horse ere it was broken.

His brows lifted in amusement. "As a connoisseur, I'll have to disagree. You are definitively a lady," he said. His voice went low with appreciation. "A very beautiful one."

Agnes hadn't known how to react. Her usually quick wit deserted her in the face of MacAllister's straightforwardness. She was used to many things, but not compliments, and she knew not how to receive one. What was it this man wanted? She'd encountered many who desired a taste of the taboo, but there was something else in MacAllister's gaze, something warm and entirely overfamiliar.

"I'm not here because James finds me beautiful." She hoped her voice didn't reveal how much he unsettled her. She had come to do business, not to be wooed. "I'm here because I speak truly of how beneficial it would be for the clans of the Highlands and the Isles to align with the king."

"Align with or follow blindly?" MacAllister challenged, although there was no venom in his words.

"You act as if there's much difference when the English threat looms over us all," Agnes retorted.

"Is the English bogeyman reason enough for my people to relinquish their pride and their autonomy? I'm sure they'll take kindly to the suggestion that they give up willingly what our ancestors have fought over for generations."

"It doesn't have to be so cut and dry," Agnes said calmly, hoping she would get through to him. "If your people were willing to negotiate, to give some sign that they would work with the king—"

"I've been well appraised of your strengths, wee ambassador—truly, I was surprised when you seemed to avoid me at all cost instead of trying to win me to your cause—but now I see why James brought you," Gareth said. His gaze was warm as he looked down at her, and the hint of a smile raised one corner of his mouth. "You're the carrot he dangles before the stubborn mule to lead it down the path he desires. Perhaps he's smarter than I imagined."

Agnes pushed off of the wall and straightened her back, surprised at his boldness and that he'd looked into her. She was used to being the one who had the upper hand in a discussion, of knowing a person's past and present peccadilloes. But MacAllister had proven to be a challenge; all she knew about him was that he was nigh on intractable, with the strength to back it up, and that he was in want of a wife to get heirs upon.

She'd tilted her head and gave him her most diplomatic smile. "I believe carrots are of a distinctly different hue, Laird MacAllister, although you're not completely mistaken in your analogy: you are most assuredly an ass. If you're done comparing me to root vegetables, I shall take my leave."

He'd smiled in that disarming way that seemed incongruous for a man of his size. "I hope our difference of opinion doesn't mean you'll begrudge me a dance," he'd said. "Or has a life at court made you too frightened of the savage Highlanders to grant me a turn?"

Agnes felt her cheeks warm with some undefined emotion. MacAllister vexed her, but it wasn't anger that his teasing stoked. "You must be forgetting yourself, laird," she replied. "We are in your lands, and here it I who is considered the savage."

He laughed, a hearty sound that drew attention in their direction. Mirth transformed his face from brooding to almost irresistible. Almost.

"It is considered quite rude to laugh so baldly at a woman, laird," Agnes said, close to losing the composure that served her well in the face of even the most boorish of courtiers. "I know things are quite different here, but I'd be remiss if I didn't inform you of your vulgarity."

His expression sobered and he gazed at her for a long moment before bowing solemnly before her. "My apologies."

Agnes thought he would bid her adieu and allow her to take her leave, but when he stood to his full height his warm hands gripped hers and pulled her close. She thought he would kiss her then, and her body responded to the possibility with anticipation instead of anger. Instead, after holding her for much longer than appropriate, he pulled her into the first steps of a reel. It took her a moment to overcome her surprise and pick up the rhythm of the minstrel's song, but once she caught it, she and Gareth moved together perfectly.

"It seems I require further instruction on the finer points of courtly interaction. You seem willing to teach me, but I find that learning is much easier when the body is engaged as well. What say you?"

His hand on her back was warm and so large that she forgot he had forced her into this dance. The heat of it was like a brand, matched by the warmth that flared in his eyes. She was distracted from any possible vexation by thoughts of what his hand would feel like on other parts of her body, how it would feel grazing her bare skin.

She had been right in keeping her distance.

"I say that a woman's leave is required *before* the dance begins, Laird MacAllister," Agnes said. She tried to be stern, but her lips refused to comply, pulling up into a smile against her wishes.

"Ah. I thought that the common method of refusal was stepping on my toe and spinning off like a top during the turn," he said. When she laughed, he smiled victoriously. There was something unnerving in his gaze, and in the way he held her as they danced. The cool, reserved places within her heated at the grip of his hand on hers, and at the way his fingers pressed into her hips instead of the light touch that was socially acceptable.

"I offer my apologies again. I laughed at the ridiculousness of our situation, not at you, Lady Agnes," he said as he moved with her, leading her effortlessly. "I'm called a savage because my people want to maintain their way of life. You're called a savage for something as ridiculous as your hue. Isn't it galling?"

His bluntness took their conversation well beyond the bounds of propriety. Even if she agreed with him, she didn't want to discuss such unpleasantness, not when she was in the arms of a man whose company she actually enjoyed. Agnes didn't share how often she felt like an outsider at court with anyone, and she wouldn't with MacAllister, even if he might be the one man who'd understand.

She laughed her false courtly laugh, the sharp, high one she used to convey that she was quite unruffled. She'd had ample opportunity to make use of it over the years. "Well, I can hardly change my situation, Laird, but surely you can reconsider parlaying with His Highness? Think of the benefits for your clansmen."

MacAllister had sighed as stepped away and guided her into a spin before pulling her close again. This dance was supposed to be chaste, but his body was a column of firm heat all along the front of her. Each accidental brush of his chest against her bosom, or his thigh against her skirts, sent a riot of sensation through her. He leaned down, his voice a rough caress of her ear that shot to her belly in a quiver of pleasure. "Do you ever permit yourself to speak of anything beyond politics? If I wanted to be bored to death with pleas for submission, I'd be dancing with one of the codgers who've been haranguing me for months."

"Sir Upton cuts a fine figure on the dance floor," Agnes said, nodding in the direction of the defense advisor whose face was so covered in wrinkles that it seemed his eyes, nose, and mouth had been lost in them. "You've chosen your partner incorrectly, if dancing was your main objective."

He'd laughed, a low and potent sound that Agnes felt in her stomach and surrounding regions. "Lady Agnes, if I told you my true objective, you wouldn't be here in my arms right now."

He hadn't had to go further than that. The way he looked at her, as if he knew her and was just discovering her at the same time, made his desires perfectly clear.

Agnes cleared her throat. "If you do not wish to speak of giving your allegiance to the king, perhaps you'd prefer we discuss the latest court gossip?" she'd asked tartly. "I wouldn't have guessed that a brave Highland chieftain would prefer discussing dress patterns and which poultice works best for a seeping wound."

"I admit I'm not very familiar with the mindset of the court and their views on certain topics," he'd said, his response lacking any hint that he knew she was mocking him. "Perhaps you can answer this question: what would the court make of two savages who fell in love?"

Agnes stiffened in his arms, and she felt a sharp, sudden pang in her chest. His earlier transgressions had been brash, but tolerable; this cut too deeply for Agnes to overlook. Could he know how they whispered behind her back? Could he sense how lonely she truly was?

"I believe the prevailing opinion is that they're not equipped to enjoy such a luxury," she said, and then some bitter part of her continued on. "Perhaps they're right. I've certainly never met a man I could love, and I don't care if I ever do."

The words felt horrid coming out of her mouth, but she would not be made fun of. If MacAllister wanted to play some cruel game with her, she would parry.

"You're mistaken, lass," he growled as he spun her in time to the music. His hands tightened, but he didn't pull her closer. Agnes ignored the pang of frustration she felt at his distance. "As repayment for your instruction on the ways of the court, I could show you how wrong you are. If that is what you wish."

She looked him full in the face, expecting to see cruel wit or, worse, a leer, but instead she was met with an earnest, searching look. His gaze on her had been hard and hot all night, but now his expression was open, as easily scannable as one of the illuminated manuscripts the king had gifted to her, and Agnes couldn't quite believe what she read there.

"Or perhaps you aren't mistaken," he said. "Perhaps you couldn't love a man. But I believe it would be quite easy for a man to care for you."

"MacAllister, what are you about?" she had asked, her breath catching in her throat. She knew it wasn't the exertion of dancing that nearly stole her words. It was her proximity to this man. Agnes finally understood why she had instinctively fled from him; he was dangerous indeed. No man had ever scared Agnes with the possibility of more, even in jest, and he had to be jesting.

"Gareth. Call me Gareth," he said. There was an urgency in his words as he leaned close to her. His name was on her lips when all hell broke loose.

A brawl erupted between two men from different clans, and it spread like wildfire. A fist missed Agnes's face by an inch before Gareth pulled her into his arms and pushed his way through the crowd. The men parted for him even as they fought, and he blocked any errant blows with his body before depositing her safely with the king's entourage. He had given her one last longing look after he placed her on her feet, and then he jumped into the fray with his hotheaded brethren.

That was the last she had seen of Gareth MacAllister, and that she thought she ever would see of him, until the Wild Knight revealed his identity before all of King James's court.

Oh, for the love of God, where is he?

Hours had passed since the tourney's end, and the MacAllister had yet to claim his kiss. Any belief that it had been simply prestige the Wild Knight sought had been discarded when she locked eyes with him after the joust had ended. There had been no mistaking the heat in his gaze, but he'd turned and left the field of battle instead of approaching the dais.

If he'd been jesting with her during their dance at his keep, he was taking it very far indeed.

At the festivities following the tournament, Agnes tried to glide easily through the crowd, as she always did, making conversation with courtiers and foreign dignitaries. There were amusements aplenty: the dark conjurers performed even more elaborate tricks, acrobats tumbled and flipped, and contortionists twisted themselves into most uncomfortable positions. But these were not the things people gossiped about. Instead, the guests spoke of the ferocious Highland chief-cum-earl, recently granted the title by James after helping to quell rebellions in the region.

Now it all came together. Agnes had heard of the arrangement in passing, but she hadn't made the connection. She, who was supposed to be on top of the political intrigues of the court.

Agnes was attempting to understand one of the Greek mathematicians who droned on and on about a theorem he'd been trying to solve for eight years solid, when a thrumming tension pressed the crowd into silence. Every guest's head turned toward the entrance, except for Agnes's. She froze mid-sentence, feeling like one who hears a storm barreling toward them across the marsh but knows there is no place to seek shelter.

Agnes felt that prickling awareness again, and turned slowly to meet her champion. Dark green eyes, the color of a moss-lined loch, fixed on her from across the room, pinning her as if MacAllister held her bodily. Everything about him was massive, from his chest and back, which were hugged by an exquisitely tailored jacket, to his muscled legs, the tanned lengths of which were visible beneath his green and yellow plaid. His dark hair was pulled back into a queue, exposing his strong jaw line and high cheekbones. His mouth was no exception to his size, wide and plump and begging to be kissed. This was no toady baron. This was the man she had dreamt of for so many months. The man she had hoped for when the Wild Knight had been nothing but a suit of armor filled with her most secret fantasy. He was here, he was stalking toward her, and she had no idea what to do.

If this were battle, her body had already submitted to cowardly defeat, ready to fall at MacAllister's feet as he plowed through the crowd, never once taking his eyes from her. Agnes took a deep breath and then gave him a smile that she hoped was steadier than her shaking hands.

She curtsied, suddenly keenly aware of the low-cut neck of her gown.

"Your Lordship—"

The words were barely out of her mouth before he was upon her. The first time they'd met, he'd availed himself of at least the rudiments of courtly behavior, this man who called himself a savage. But now his hands gripped her by Agnes waist, shocking her with their brute strength before he pulled her toward him. She was no small woman, but she felt like a sprite pressed against the solid mass of the Highland earl.

"I believe I asked you to call me Gareth," he reminded her in a voice that was barely more than a growl, and she didn't know what to do but obey.

"Gareth," she breathed, finally, and then his head dipped down and his lips brushed hers, completely clearing Agnes's mind of the proper etiquette for rebuffing an admirer in the middle of a banquet. His lips were warm and firm, but softer than she ever could have imagined as they glided against hers. When she'd been told that she'd have to kiss the winner of the tourney, she'd expected to provide a quick peck, but Gareth wasn't interested in claiming such a paltry prize. There was no mistaking the fact that he was claiming *her*, branding her with the heat and power of his mouth and tongue, running his hands over her back as he pulled her closer against the solid warmth of his body. He was making her his.

In front of the entire court.

Agnes tried to pull away, tried to protest, but when she opened her mouth his tongue slipped in, warm and slick and overpowering. He crushed her to his body as he pillaged her mouth, close enough that she could feel his heart beating steadily in his chest. The hoots and cheers of the crowd around them faded into so much background noise as Agnes gave herself completely to his kiss. There was only his mouth, the sweet, malty taste of him, and his hands as they slid down to cup her ass.

"The Earl of Arran provided marvelous entertainment these three days of tourney, and now that he has claimed his prize, we shall dine!" Queen Margaret's voice rang out, waking Agnes from her daze. Two dainty hands slipped in between her and Gareth and pried them apart; the queen was surprisingly strong.

How long had they stood there pressed against one another, a spectacle for all to see? Agnes didn't know, and she found that she didn't care either. The need that had been simmering since she first locked eyes with Gareth at his keep was now at full boil. It hadn't been a fluke or a passing fancy all those months ago. She wanted this man, and he wanted her, too.

Margaret slipped her arm through Agnes's, tugging her gently, but pointedly, away from Gareth.

"Your Lordship, I know that this title is new to you, but one of the more enforced rules of the peerage is that one doesn't perform sexual congress, or near it, at the dining table," Margaret said sweetly over her shoulder. "You are seated next to Agnes, but I will dump a cup of ale over your head if you continue to behave like a canine in heat. That goes for you too, sweet Agnes."

Agnes wanted to sink beneath the flagstones and never see the light of day again, she was so embarrassed. More than that, she wanted to feel Gareth's mouth against hers once more, to memorize how his lips moved and the intricate patterns his tongue traced against hers.

Instead, she nodded demurely and followed the queen to the table of honor. She was tempted to ask Margaret if she, too, felt the pressure of Gareth's stare on her back, but she kept the question to herself.

Agnes tried to ignore the heat radiating from the chair to her left as she picked at her meal, but Gareth was so close and her mind kept seeking out the memory of their kiss, unbidden. She still reeled from it, although hours had passed since he'd crushed her to his body. His kiss had been powerful, but not just because of the brute strength of him. There had been emotion in the joining of their mouths. His lips and tongue had conveyed a message that words could not, one that spoke of longing and passion and something that touched her more deeply than both of those things.

She wanted to talk to him, to know more of him, but instead she made idle conversation with the various dignitaries and men who had fought in the tourney, answering their questions about her experiences at James's court. That was easier than dealing with the feelings Gareth stirred in her. Her fantasy had come true when her champion had been revealed, but now what? He would return to his clanspeople and she would be left with nothing but an even more acute knowledge of what she was losing.

"Would you like more wine?" Gareth's velvety burr ended the silence between them. He had addressed her directly, and she could no longer protect herself by pretending he wasn't there.

She turned to see him holding a flagon toward her cup solicitously, as if she hadn't been carefully ignoring him for most of the evening. His gaze on her was a living thing, like the fire licking at the wood in the hearth.

"You are the visitor here, Your Lordship," she said, trying to keep her voice even-keeled. The consummate hostess. "It is I who should be serving you."

His eyes went dark at her words.

"Do you wish to serve me?" he asked in a low voice, leaning closer to her. "Because I do not require a wench to do my bidding. What I desire is that which would give you pleasure. If this wine gives you pleasure, I will pour it. If there is something else you would ask of me, it is yours."

"Your Lordship—"

"Gareth." His reminder cut her off, and she was glad of it because she knew not how to respond.

"Gareth, what do you want of me?" she asked.

"Perhaps more than is advisable," he said, studying her face. He placed the flagon down on the table. "I told myself that I came to this tourney simply to benefit my people, but that was a lie. I admit, before you came to my keep, I was intrigued by the tales of my fellow clansmen of the rare beauty who parlayed like the veriest statesman at the behest of the king. I was supposed to be searching for a bride, but instead I sought to learn more about you.

"Then I saw you with James's retinue and I had no choice in the matter, really. I wanted you, and a dance wasn't enough. When I heard about the tourney, I thought it was a sign." He shook his head, flashed her a smile that seemed to strike her a direct blow, stealing her breath away. "It is entirely foolish, and I'd laugh at myself if I weren't in such agony. Did you feel it, too, all those months ago?"

"I know not of what you speak," Agnes said, looking away from him before he could catch her untruth. Her heart pounded and her dress suddenly felt too small around her chest, constricting her breath.

"For weeks after we danced, I believed the rumors that you were a changeling," he said in a low voice, pitched only for her ears beneath the tumult of the evening's festivities. He took her hand in his, and Agnes trembled at the intimacy of the act. "I dreamt of you. I longed for your scent, which laced my jacket, to perfume my bed sheets. I believed it had to be some Sidhe curse to need a woman so badly."

"Need?" Agnes repeated. The word felt foreign in a way that Gaelic did not, that English did not, although neither was her mother tongue. It could mean many things, this simple word. She had expected that he would want her or desire her; need was a different thing entirely. It was what spurred a surge of envy when she saw how smitten James was with Margaret. It was what left her feeling hollowed out and empty when she clambered into her lonely bed every night.

"Your Lordship, I think you mistake simple infatuation for something more," she said, unable to meet his intense gaze. She knew if she looked at him she might believe him, and she could not afford to lose herself so easily.

Gareth's hand grazed her chin, nudging her head up so that she was looking him full in the face. "Do I look like a man who is easily mistaken?"

Agnes's senses took leave of her. She was like one of the king's guard, whose vision was restricted to the thin slit in their armor that allowed them to see the road ahead; she feared what obstacles lay just outside her view if she chose to believe Gareth's words. What could become of such a pairing? Had Gareth given any thought to what his people, and the world, would make of them?

"The poet Dunbar recited some verse yesterday evening after the meal," she said quietly. "Were you privy to his words?"

"No," Gareth said, obviously confused. "I find Dunbar is not quite my taste. What poem is this, that captured your attention?"

"'Why were you blinded, Reason? Why, alas!'" she began, trying to say the words with ease, as if she were simply recounting the poem to any visitor to the court. She pulled her hand from his. "'And made a hell appear as my paradise, and mercy seem where I found no grace.'"

"Hell? You fear I do not speak truly." Gareth gave her another assessing look and his features softened. "Or perhaps you are more afraid that I do?"

Agnes felt exposed, but she could not deny his words.

"Come! Give us the truth and put these rumors to an end," a slurred voice interrupted jovially, cutting the through the din of the hall and the illusion of privacy Agnes had felt when speaking with Gareth. "I would know your origins. What type of wench are you? Were you trained to give your master pleasure?"

Humiliation scoured Agnes from head to toe. Most people weren't indelicate enough to bring up the more horrid things they'd heard about her past, especially not to her face, but the oafish English knight had imbibed too deeply and shouted his indiscreet question across the table.

Agnes struggled for something politic to say, something witty to gloss over this scene and continue the festivities as if she hadn't been degraded before everyone in earshot. But then the feet of Gareth's chair scraped against the stone floor as he stood, hand resting on the hilt of his short sword.

"The tourney was held in honor of this maiden. You fought to be her champion, yet you think nothing of asking such crude questions of her?" Gareth's voice was low, but powerful enough to be heard over the clamor. Silence began to spread over the guests like a plague as they realized someone had run afoul of the Wild Knight.

The English boor, however, was still unaware that he had caused offense.

"Well, you must be curious too, with the way you had at her earlier," the man said with a laugh. "Come now, she doesn't mind my asking. Why would she?"

Anger roiled in Agnes's stomach. For the most part, people were kind to her even if they were curious. But there were always those who thought her dark skin inured her to insult. She always had to be graceful in her put-downs and repulsions—that was one of the concessions she made to her position in the court—but oh, how it vexed her. Gareth, however, had no such graciousness, and Agnes was glad of that when he bounded straight over the table and grabbed the English bastard by the throat. The man was bowled back out of his seat, but Gareth maintained his hold, landing in a crouch beside the man and squeezing harder.

"As we're asking idiotic questions, are you able to breathe through your arse? You might have need of such a skill after I bash your bloody face in."

"Highland savage," the chemist from London beside her sneered, and Agnes knew he only said aloud what several people were thinking. The faces of the courtiers lining the table ranged from horrified to intrigued, but Agnes covered her mouth to hide the inappropriate smile that pulled at her lips. He had been so gentle with her that she had nearly forgotten his reputation. She didn't wish death upon the Englishman, but Gareth's readiness to defend her honor warmed that loneliest part of her heart. It was...sweet.

"Jamie, do something!" Queen Margaret chided her husband from the head of the table, although both she and the king seemed to be quite amused by the spectacle. One less Englishman wouldn't be such an incredible crime against humanity in their eyes.

The king stood abruptly, snapping his fingers at Gareth to get his attention. "I believe this is a sign that the festivities have reached their conclusion. If MacAllister would take his seat, via the floor so he doesn't plant his foot in the mutton again, we can proceed with the finale of this banquet."

Gareth ignored the king as the knight flailed in his grip. The Englishman's face was a frightening shade of red, and Agnes began to worry. If Gareth was really set on murdering someone for her, there were other men who had caused her much greater offense.

"Please let him go, Your Lordship," Agnes called out, to no effect. "Gareth! Release him. I beg of you."

The English knave collapsed to the floor in a gasping heap, and Gareth stared down at him. "When you can speak again, you'll apologize to the lass," he said.

The man managed a sound approximating a duck's quack, but an affirmative one. He crawled away, glancing over his shoulder as if he feared that Gareth would come at him again.

"I give you my thanks," Agnes said quietly when Gareth took his seat. She wanted to touch him, to pull him close and calm the flood of feeling rising within her, but instead she placed her hands in her lap.

"I will always champion you," he said simply. "If you will have me."

What did those words mean? Agnes's heart was pounding, and she would never have admitted it, but in addition to the knot of emotion in her chest there was dampness between her thighs. Seeing Gareth propel himself toward the Englishman, the fierceness in his every movement utilized for the protection of her honor, had touched upon something innate and undeniably attractive. His plaid had flown up when he'd leapt across the table, revealing a muscular ass and the hint of something thick and veined. She wondered if he could possibly be that large or if it had been the play of shadow and light, but then again, everything about the man was oversized.

She realized she had been staring at him as she ruminated on his endowment. Her thoughts must have been plain, for the corner of Gareth's lips lifted into a smug grin. It was the first time she had seen a smile grace his face since he had arrived at the banquet, and she remembered that, somehow, it was possible for him to be even more handsome.

"Are you afraid of heights?" he asked, and the question was so ridiculous given all that had just happened that she burst out laughing.

"What would possess you to ask such a thing?" she asked, right as James raised his glass and called out, "Adieu to our lovely Agnes and her unrelenting champion, the Earl of Arran!"

The area around the table of honor erupted in a frenzy of motion. The acrobats who had worked the crowd earlier now flipped and tumbled toward Agnes and Gareth. The conjurers in their hooded robes converged on them, too, one blowing fire from his mouth. Agnes had been frightened of the tattooed men, but one of them winked at her as he dropped some kind of device at their feet, and she winked back. Pungent smoke billowed out of the small object, obscuring everything around them. Agnes couldn't see, but two strong hands gripped her by the arms and pulled her onto Gareth's lap. For a moment she was so distracted by his hard chest against her back, by his muscular thighs and the rigid length pressing against her buttocks, that she didn't realize they were moving. Vertically.

"James had my chair rigged with ropes for the grand finale," he said into her ear. His words were nearly lost in the shouts of amazement from the crowd.

Of course he did, Agnes thought, wishing it weren't a crime to throttle royalty.

They were being pulled through the air, and the feeling of flying was as exhilarating as it was frightening. Maybe she wouldn't commit regicide. Gareth held her tightly to him with one hand; his other hand was situated between her legs where he gripped the seat of the chair.

The trip was so quick that Agnes didn't have time to panic. Only when the chair legs touched the ground and her feet didn't, when Gareth held fast to her instead of letting her go, did her head start to spin. They were now ensconced in the darkness of the rampart that ringed the high-ceilinged hall of the castle.

"I'm pleased James is such a showman," Gareth said, his burr tickling her ear. He smelled of whisky and the masculine soap she'd had the alchemist make for the baths of visiting statesmen.

"Why?" she asked. One of his forearms still rested between her thighs as he gripped the seat, a heavy length that seemed to be only slightly thicker than the one pressing into her from behind. When he moved it away, her legs squeezed shut, missing the warmth.

"Because it has given me the chance to do this," he said. His hand spread flat on her stomach, holding her in place as he moved his lips over the shell of her ear and down her neck. The trail of kisses sent shocks of pleasure through Agnes. A sweet ache bloomed in her belly, and the peaks of her breasts tightened beneath the fine fabric of her gown.

In the hall below them, Agnes could hear the shouts of surprise and delight as the smoke cleared and guests realized they had disappeared. Not much light reached this far up in the great hall; they were shielded from view, and it seemed to the guests that they had simply vanished. To them, it was an act of magic, not a mechanical wonder of the king's devising.

The noise of the hundreds of revelers conjecturing on their departure grew louder, obscuring the whimpers Gareth's questing mouth drew from her as it explored her sensitive skin. She was finally alone with her green-eyed Highlander. His mouth was on hers, his hands roamed her body, and desire heated her blood.

"I haven't been able to stop thinking of you, Agnes." He said her name reverently. "When faced with matters of import, I wondered what your quick mind what make of them. When I ate sugared berries, I wondered if they were as sweet as your lips. I conjured what your laugh would sound like as you lay stretched across my bed, sated. And I couldn't stop imagining how warm and tight you would be when I was sheathed inside of you."

Agnes knew that such boldness was uncouth, but Gareth's confession thrilled her. From the first moment she'd seen him, she'd craved his touch, and when she'd spoken to him his candor and humor had intrigued her. His words now, the honesty of them and the import, nestled around the dream of her heart like the rich soil in the castle gardens.

She could feel his cock throbbing through the layers of her gown, each pulse receiving an answering flutter from her sex. She was wet for him, and her slick pearl ached for his caress. She'd only had a few sips of the strong wine, but she felt drunk on the possibility that lay before her.

"Gareth," she said, reaching her arm behind her to stroke his hair, arching her body in the process. "Please touch me."

He shuddered, exhaling forcefully as he stroked his hands over her torso. He slid them up under her breasts, and she wished heavy fabric wasn't shielding her from his caresses. Her fingers sank into his hair and he rubbed his stubbled cheek against the sensitive skin of her inner wrist. She gasped at the sensation that bolted through her. How would that stubble feel elsewhere?

"Are you sure, lass?" he asked.

"Yes," she said, rocking impatiently in his.

"You should know that your bedding me comes with certain responsibilities," he said, his fingers sliding up and rolling her stiffened nipples between his fingers. Even through her dress, it felt exquisite.

"Such as?" she asked, trying to keep her voice calm as erotic bliss thrummed in her body. She arched her back to press her breasts into his calloused hands, and he rumbled a laugh from behind her.

One hand left her breast to begin tugging up her skirts. "Such as your agreeing to be my wife," he said.

Agnes froze just before a cry of pleasure escaped her lips. The rigid thrust of her breast up into his palm eased, and she sank back against him.

"I beg your pardon, Your Lordship?" she said. She knew some men would say anything in the heat of passion, and she accredited his words to that. "'Tis a very extreme price for a tumble. Is marriage required of every woman you bed?"

"Nay, just you, Agnes." His words were thick with some kind of emotion, and she regretted that she couldn't see his face.

"Gareth, I don't understand." For a moment she felt as she was still suspended in the air, but without the safety of Gareth's arms around her.

"You of all people know that I'm wanting for a wife. I hadn't been overeager to make that reality, but when I met you, everything fell into place. Over the past few months, I've endeavored to make myself a better man," he said as his hand finally reached beneath the raised hem of her skirt, brushing the soft skin of her thighs before cupping her mound. He didn't move, but the warm heft of his hand against her slit was enough to make her squirm. "For my people, and for you. The improvements to my keep, the truces with neighboring clans, this bloody earlship—all done in the hopes that they'd be enough to compel you to come home with me. To share my life."

Tears sprang to her eyes. She felt completely unstrung: the only man who had ever truly moved her was bringing her pleasure at his hand while asking her to be his wife.

"You know nothing about me except for rumor and innuendo," she countered. "How can you want a life with someone you do not know?"

"Do not feign ignorance, Agnes," he said, unconsciously echoing Margaret's words. His hands on her were gentle, although his voice was strained. "Most men know nothing of their wife on their wedding day beyond the fact that she can sew and play a pretty tune. When we danced was the first time I ever felt a true connection with a woman. I knew then I wanted you in my bed; 'twas after you left, after I wanted to tear down the stone walls with frustration, that I knew I wanted you for a wife. I was coming for you, Agnes, tournament or no. It doesn't hurt that I got to display my skills for you, though. James isn't the only showman."

His warm breath tickled her neck, but she was still too shocked to register it. Her heart had been as desolate as the bogs surrounding the castle for so long that she couldn't imagine it ever being otherwise. Now, here was a man she had dreamt of asking for her hand. "It wouldn't be prudent to believe a word you say," she whispered. "It's not done, such a marriage. What if I say no?"

"I willna lie: I was hoping that would be the case," Gareth said, and Agnes's stomach dropped with disappointment. She'd wanted his plea to be true more than she'd realized. More than anything.

Gareth nipped at her neck, sending a surge of heat through her body, before continuing. "That means I'll have to convince you."

The hand resting at her apex began to move, his thick fingers sliding to press against her with the perfect amount of pressure. He touched her like he had already traversed her body, had mapped out the most direct roads and hidden paths to her ecstasy. There was no tentativeness, no guessing, in his touch, and Agnes took her pleasure in his surety.

His fingers drifted down to her opening and he worked one in slowly, knuckle by knuckle, the sensation so sharp that Agnes bucked in his lap. Another thick finger followed, and Agnes was lost to their shared desire as he stroked her from within, his fingers curling as if beckoning her. She squeezed him, clenching tightly around his digits as pleasure enveloped her like the mist on the moors. Her breath came faster as she moved on his hand. She was so close, the sensation threatening to overwhelm her—

He pulled his hand away abruptly, her sudden emptiness a shock that verged on anger.

Gareth's hand cupped her face, turned it so that she was staring back at him. The intensity of his gaze was scouring, making her feel he had cut through all the layers and was looking at the real her: the scared girl who had cried for her parents as the cold waters of a strange continent flooded the hold of the slave ship, and the lonely woman that girl had become. It was freeing, to have a man gaze at her like he knew everything about her and also like he'd want her even if she never shared that ancient angst with him.

"Still no?" he asked, challenge in his tone.

"I believe I need further convincing," she said. Her words rode a rough gasp. His hand left her face, but she continued to look back at him as he grabbed her at the waist and lifted her easily. She held his gaze as she pushed her bulky skirts out from between them, along with his plaid, and reached for his rigid member. She used her knees against his thighs to maneuver herself until the wide, flared tip of him nudged at her opening.

Gareth bought his mouth to hers as he thrust up into her, slowly. His tongue slid over hers as the pressure of his girth spread her from within, his pace inexorable. His hips and his hands at her waist controlled the rhythm, lifting and raising her. His teeth nipped at her lips as his cock filled her completely, stretching her to the limit between pleasure and pain.

Agnes rocked in his lap as she adjusted to him, returning his kisses as she swiveled her hips to match his pace. They were quiet now, but his words were transmuted into the most ancient code, shared by the press of lips and the clash of tongues. When he kissed her, he was revealing some secret part of himself, and that same message was encoded into the pumping of his hips and the way his cock throbbed when she kissed him without inhibition. He seemed to be seeking something from her even as he gave. Agnes couldn't focus, couldn't think, his hidden message lost as her release rushed at her from all angles, a merciless opponent ready to fell her.

"My Agnes," he groaned as he thrust up into her. "So perfect. Say yes."

A bliss bordering on agony enveloped Agnes, the delicious pleasure spreading from her sex to her curled toes and crabbed fingers. But she would not yield so easily. "Not yet," she moaned.

"I'll ask one more time, Agnes. Will ye be my wife?" He pumped into her with renewed vigor, his ass lifting them up off the chair with the force of his efforts. The friction was unbearable, and her inner walls clamped tightly around his cock.

His hand slipped between her legs, moving over her slickness in a gentle way that was almost loving.

Loving.

That was the hidden message. It wasn't lust or desire. It was love.

"Will you?" he asked again. His voice was strained from withholding his release, and Agnes thought she sensed uncertainty there as well.

"Yes!" Agnes cried out her acceptance as the orgasm crashed through her battlements, overwhelming her defenses with wave after wave of bliss. She gasped for air, head thrown back on his shoulder as her body clenched and trembled. Gareth pressed his mouth against her neck and groaned his release as he shuddered beneath her.

They were quiet for a long moment, the sounds of the revelry below drowning out their heaving breaths.

"And here I thought I knew all the best way to get an opponent to bend to your will," she said. "I may have to incorporate this technique into my repertoire. There are a lot of savage Highlanders out there who need to be cajoled."

Gareth grunted before standing and cradling her in his arms. "I appreciate your acumen, but the only thing I ask of ye as a wife is that such cajoling be reserved for only one clansmen."

"The McPherson?" she asked, laughing as he scowled at the mention of a rival clansmen. He kissed her roughly as he carried her along the ramparts toward the door that would lead them to the guest wing of the castle. She knew she should be worried, but all she felt was safe.

"I knew you were going to be a handful," he said, and he seemed quite happy about it. "Now, let's try that in a bed, wife."

EPILOGUE

Four weeks had passed since the night when Gareth had claimed her on the ramparts. Because she was prudent, she reminded him that a vow made under duress, even exquisite duress, wasn't the best foundation for a happy life together; she bade him woo her, and he did, showing that his renowned stubbornness could be applied to more than confounding his rivals.

They had tried "that" in her bed, and in the great hall, and under a flowering pear tree in the palatial gardens, and each time had been better than the last. Gareth was a talented lover, to be sure, but more than that, he was a sensitive one. He cared for her, and to Agnes's great relief it was not a joke. The love between them grew and grew, making her think of a theorem one of the mathematicians among the exotics had tried to explain to her once. The man had described numbers that multiplied exponentially without any possible end in sight. That was how her feelings for Gareth grew: exponentially.

Sometimes she felt so full of happiness she worried that she might simply burst, like the monstrous haggis that had been presented to her that first night at the MacAllister's keep; her new home.

She shifted in the silken sheets of the huge bed she shared with her husband, grimacing at the memory. She liked offal as much as the next woman, but it had been quite too much. Her new subjects had looked on eagerly and she hadn't wanted to disappoint, so she'd eaten the whole thing in one sitting. That feat had gained her a host of admirers—and an intimate relationship with the keep's apothecary, who'd spent the next few days tending to her upset stomach.

"What vexes you, wife?" a deep voice rumbled from across the room. She hadn't heard Gareth return from his morning duties. The room was a drafty stone square, but it was hung with tapestries that both kept it warm and dampened sound—something very useful to the newlyweds.

Agnes placed her hands over her stomach as she remembered the horrid pain her desire to please her new people had caused her.

Gareth was removing his boots, but he froze in place, a strange expression on his face as his eyes lingered on her stomach.

"You're not...we're not..."

She looked down at her hands; they mimicked that of an expectant mother. A peal of laughter escaped her and she dropped back onto the thick mattress. Not more than a few seconds passed before Gareth's weight was upon her, pressing her further down into the bed.

"Well?" he prodded. His gaze was intense and his body hard and hot beneath his plaid. His chest was bare and the coarse hair there scraped against her own exposed skin.

"We've just married, Gareth," she said. "I know you're considered quite as virile as they come, but I think it's a bit too soon for that."

His face relaxed in relief, and all of Agnes's laughter died in her.

"Do you not want bairns?" she asked carefully. She left out the portion of her question that had wedged a shard of fear in her heart. *With me?* She'd forgotten what it was to have a family linked by blood, but she wished to experience it again one day.

Gareth's hands cradled her face, gentle as always although she'd seen him toss a caber near to the moon.

"I want you to have our children more than almost anything," he said in a low burr. His lips brushed against hers softly. "I hope they have your eyes and your intelligence and your kindness. But more than that, I want more time…I'm not ready to share ye quite yet, Agnes MacAllister."

"Oh," she said, again at a lack for words. She had once harbored fantasies about Gareth, but now that he was hers she realized her imagination could never capture all the wonderful facets of the real man.

His lips brushed hers again, the grazing of tender skin spreading a familiar warmth through Agnes's body.

"That's not to say we should stop practicing," he said with a mischievous grin.

Their lips met in a passionate kiss, and the evidence of his arousal pressed against her. Agnes tried to think of the court etiquette for dealing with a handsome husband who loved her dearly and was well on his way to giving her a thorough bedding, but instead did as her heart desired.

"About that, we are in full agreement, husband," she replied, grasping at his plaid.

After that, there was only the delicious weight of him pressing her into the bed, and the love that thrummed in her veins and his.

AUTHOR'S NOTE

The setting of this story, The Tournament of the Black Lady, is based on The Tournament of the Wild Knight and the Black Lady, which took place in Edinburgh in 1507 and 1508.

The following texts were helpful in the writing of this story:

- Women and Race in Early Modern Texts, by Joyce Green MacDonald. (2002. Cambridge University Press.)
- (Blacks in) 'Tudor Britain.' In The Oxford Companion to Black British History. eds. D. Dabydeen, J. Gilmore and C. Jones. (2007. Oxford University Press.)

ABOUT THE AUTHOR

Alyssa Cole is a science editor, pop culture nerd, and romance junkie who lives in the Caribbean and occasionally returns to her fast-paced NYC life. When she's not busy writing, traveling, and learning French, she can be found watching anime with her real-life romance hero or tending to her herd of animals.

Contact her on

@alyssacolelit

Facebook.com/ AlyssaColeLit

www.AlyssaCole.com